Mud Witch Boy of Ghost Canyon

Story and Drawings by
Valerie Temple

Outskirts Press, Inc.
Denver, Colorado

Mud Witch Boy of Ghost Canyon
All Rights Reserved.
Copyright © 2009 Valerie Temple
v3.0

Outskirts Press, Inc.
http://www.outskirtspress.com

ISBN PB: 978-1-4327-3103-8
ISBN HB: 978-1-4327-1133-7

Library of Congress Control Number: 2009920267

Outskirts Press and the "OP" logo are trademarks belonging to Outskirts Press, Inc.

PRINTED IN THE UNITED STATES OF AMERICA

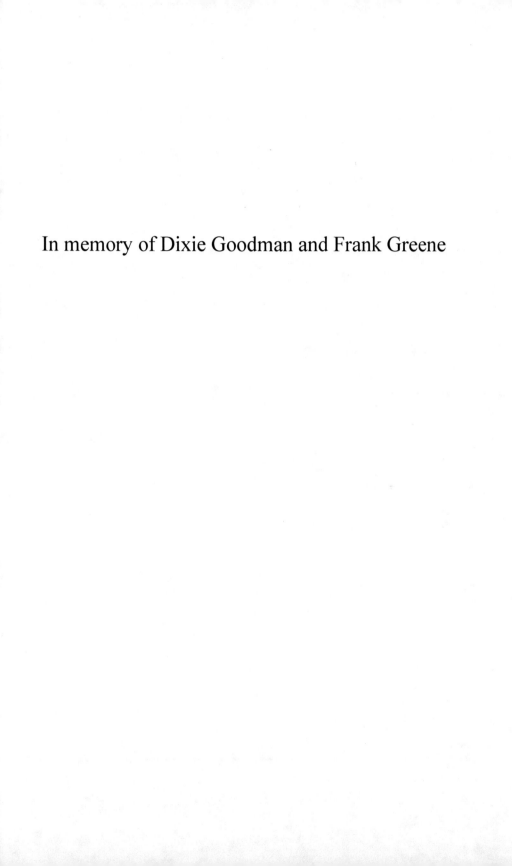

In memory of Dixie Goodman and Frank Greene

Mud Witch Boy of Ghost Canyon is dedicated to my mother, Rella, and all my family and friends who have read, edited, and believed in my story. Thank you Mom, Dixie, Frank, Pat, Claudia, Jane, Lorraine Chuck, Chucky, Dale, Nikki, Dad, Anita, Gloria, Wayne, Omar, Wimpy, Fledermouse, Pooh Bear, Quiche, Keiko, Kashibu, Pheister, and Julio.

Acknowledgements

A special thank you to:
Writing Consultant Catherine Ann Jones,
www.wayofstory.com

Table of Contents

Preface

Chapter 1   1
The Sacred Cottonwood Grove

Chapter 2   6
Dream Spirits

Chapter 3   15
The Stranger from Ghost Canyon

Chapter 4   24
Child of Prairie Mud

Chapter 5   32
The Story of Swallow Tail

Chapter 6   43
The Hunting Trip

Chapter 7   56
The Path of Mud-Clay

Chapter 8   67
Broken Shards and Animal Tracks

Chapter 9   76
A Voice in the Wilderness

Chapter 10   89
Child of Stardust and Prairie Mud

Epilogue   95

Mud Boy's Alphabet   97

Job 12: 7-13   99

About the Author   101

Preface

There was a time when giant cottonwood trees grew as far as you could see. They were so big that their branches disappeared way up into the sky, connecting them to the heavens. Now only one remains. It sits high up in the canyon where a river tumbles down a rocky winding path through its roots. Water collects into a clay pond sheltered by the giant cottonwood, then makes its way down the canyon. The first people—the cave-dwelling people—lived in the canyons creating images and symbols on the rock surface. You can even see them today.

A figure riding a dog-like creature is etched high upon the canyon walls. Ancient pot shards show the same mysterious images. But not even the storyteller Dreaming Bear can tell you what these images mean or the story behind them. When the people lost their dreams, they forgot how to read the signs and images.

The Old Ones tell of the time when every night they had dreams. They dreamed stories about how to survive and how to live peacefully with the animals and the rest of the earth.

The animals have not forgotten. The animals know all the mysteries of the earth. They never forget. They have a wisdom that helped keep the people alive. The elders called this knowledge "Animal Wisdom"— the wisdom the people learned from their dreams and by observing the animals of the earth.

But because the people prospered and lived successfully up in the canyon, they felt they had no use for the animals, other than to eat them when hungry.

So one day the Dream Spirits quit sending the people dreams and gave them nightmares instead. That was when the people forgot how to read the signs and symbols. They forgot their stories. They forgot Animal Wisdom.

Chapter 1

The Sacred Cottonwood Grove

Child of Prairie Mud
Come down from the Canyon,
Down to the River in your boat made of Willow.
Gently the waves rock to and fro,
And Winds from the Cottonwood sing you to
sleep.

Red Fox is howling, "Come ride with me,
Little feral child of the Canyon,
Let us sing of the stories, let us sing the Dream
Song.
Let us never forget every creature created,
They all have a story to tell."

Sister Bobcat, Brother Coyote,
Teach us the hunt in need to survive,
Rabbit and Deer surrender their life so we may live.

Cousins Beaver and Otter,
Show us the magic of work and of play,
While Grandfather Bear dreams deep in a cave.

Grandmother Meadowlark gives us the gift of
song.
Swallow Tail shows us the Path of Mud-Clay.
We all walk together,
In the Sacred Cottonwood Grove,
We all walk together,
On this Earth we call home.

Don't be afraid little child of the Canyon,
We are your family, Believe in yourself,
You bring the Dreams of Animal Wisdom,
You bring the Dreams to all who believe.

Strikes of lightning silhouetted the giant cottonwood tree high up in Ghost Canyon. The jagged brilliance lit up the whole night sky. Something way up in the lofty tree branches began to rustle. And from what looked like an enormous nest, a creature of some sort began to stir and crawl out upon the limb, hesitating a moment then letting out a high-pitched squeal. Two more squeals burst forth, with long pauses in between. Then suddenly the creature darted down to a limb where an object hung whipping wildly in the wind. Quickly it took the object from the limb and strapped it to its back. Awkwardly it made its way, slipping and stumbling down the wet limbs of the tree.

Before it could reach the lower limbs, another strike of lightning hit with a fierce and cracking blow—a blow too close to the unsuspecting creature. The creature, and the object it carried, were swept away by the wind. Tossing about in midair, it struggled to hold onto the object, and falling… falling…falling it fell to the soggy ground below.

There was a long and uncomfortable stillness that lay with the small lifeless heap below the giant cottonwood tree. No more sound, no more movements. And as quickly as the rain began, it now ended.

The morning sun began to color the sky with startling oranges and blood reds, spreading into the flow of the river. The giant cottonwood tree as well as the whole canyon seemed to breathe a sigh of relief as the fallen heap began to stir. Into the flow of the river the creature floated. The object the creature held during its almost fatal fall now served as some kind of boat. And that boat carried it safely down the winding river, away from the canyon, away from the giant cottonwood tree.

The river seemed to know just where to take the boat with its sleeping passenger. It whirled around big boulders; it danced upon the waves of the water. And when the boat and creature finished making its way down the winding canyon, it floated peacefully with the lazy river out onto the flat prairie. The fading colors from the morning sun gradually gave way to the blues of the sky and the greens from the willows that lined the shore. The boat continued down the river, pausing only briefly now and then in the shallows…then going on.

Suddenly the creature popped its head from the boat when it heard strange sounds. Quickly it paddled into the safety of the willows.

Chapter 2

Dream Spirits

High upon tip-top most,
Branches reach for stars above.
They hold within their loving arms,
The Dream Stars sent from Heaven.

Cautiously the creature looked out from the willows and listened closely.

"What are dreams?" Wander asked as she and her friend Little Otter watched their hands making circles in the river water. She had overheard the elders talk about this word only once before and was curious. The "dream" word had always been hushed, brushed aside by the other adults. Was it a bad word? Its mysteriousness made it all the more curious.

"Dreams are stories we have while we are asleep," one of the elders explained. "Our people once believed that dreams came from the stars created by Great Spirit. The stars collected high up in the giant cottonwood tree branches."

"Yes, and the Dream Spirits used to live up in those trees, frolicking with the animals of the canyon," commented another elder.

"What are Dream Spirits?" Little Otter asked, looking up at the elder with a puzzled expression on her face.

"Dream Spirits are small invisible creatures only the animals can see. The Dream Spirits lived in harmony like brothers and sisters with all of the animals of the earth. They were the ones who used to bring dream stories from the stars to our people."

"Yeah, old man, but what do the Dream Spirits bring us now?" a young man yelled out as he passed by. "Nothing but horrible nightmares." He scowled at the older people sitting by the river then hurried away.

The creature quickly hid under its boat, frightened by the angry sound that came from the young man.

The elder focused his attention on the few children playing at the water's edge.

"At night the Dream Spirits drifted from branch to branch gathering up dreams from the stars. When everyone was asleep, they would pass the dreams out to all the people and animals. But this was long ago when the animals and people walked together in the Sacred Cottonwood Grove."

The creature settled back into its boat, still hidden by the willows but comfortable now with the gentle voices of the elders.

"This was the time when animals were no less than people and they could talk with one another. They even went to the same place to dream together," another elder added. The oldest man, Dreaming Bear, frowned and got up stiffly, hanging heavily on an ancient piece of a cottonwood bough. He had been listening, yet had not said a single word.

"What say you, Dreaming Bear? Why do you leave just now?"

"Please…stay awhile longer. No one tells the story as well as you."

"Yes, we need to keep the stories alive so Animal Wisdom will not die."

When Dreaming Bear began to speak the creature moved closer and peeked out of the willows. Taking particular notice of the old man, it began to listen even more carefully than before.

"Like the rest of our people I too no longer have dreams. I only know what was so a long time ago. It becomes harder for me to remember the older I get. It is the young ones that the stories must be passed down to now. But the mothers and fathers of our children do not listen. They have made their own children afraid to listen."

"I am not afraid to listen," one boy yelled out. He jumped upon a boulder to make himself look bigger.

"My father is Hungry Hunter. He is the bravest man in the whole village. I will be just like him when I grow up. I am not afraid of anything!"

"It will take someone brave like you, Spotted Eagle, to bring back our dreams of Animal Wisdom," Dreaming Bear replied thoughtfully. He sat back down and faced the group of listeners.

10

"The only way to bring back the dreams is for someone to get past the angry ghost animals up in the canyon—someone brave and strong enough to climb the last and only giant cottonwood tree and find the lost Dream Spirit. The Dream Spirit would then have to be convinced we are worthy to have our dreams back."

"Why did our people stop believing in dreams?" Wander asked as she got out of the water and sat on a rock near Dreaming Bear.

"Dreams weren't something they could hold in their hands. Dreams weren't something they could eat or even something they could own. Having everything they wanted, they felt the dreams were unnecessary. So in time they quit believing in their dreams. But dreams no longer have meaning, nor do they have power when people quit believing in them. So instead of bringing dreams to our cave-dwelling ancestors of the canyon, the Dream Spirits brought nightmares."

"Why don't our people live in the canyon like our ancestors?" asked Spotted Eagle.

"Because when the people quit believing in their dreams bad things began to happen. By cutting or burning down the cottonwood trees up in the canyon and along the river, the people thought they would get rid of their nightmares. The Dream

Spirits became endangered as their habitat was quickly destroyed.

"Then one night while the people slept high up in their homes in the canyon caves, Great Spirit sent a star full of dreams from the heavens. The star searched desperately for a tree in which to land. Before it could reach the last standing cottonwood tree, it crashed to the earth into a fiery cloud of star dust. The thunderous explosion could be heard for miles around. Terrified people and animals quickly fled the canyon never to return.

"The fire that came from the explosion burned up everything in the canyon except for one tree, the giant sacred cottonwood tree. The sky was dark both day and night for several weeks. So black and smoky was the sky that not a single star could be seen anywhere.

"The people and animals who escaped from the canyon, never dared to return. The canyon became taboo. They say those who did not make it out alive became ghosts and cry for their family to come and take them away from the dreaded canyon. You can hear these cries even today.

"Now all that is left in the canyon are angry ghost animals. The people have never returned to the canyon because they believe the ghost animals want revenge for destroying their beloved Dream Spirits. This is why even today, we do not go near the canyon. That is…except for Wander's grandmother, Meadow Lark, the old clay woman who digs for clay." Dreaming Bear nodded towards Wander and smiled.

"Spotted Eagle," his mother cried out, "I thought I told you and Little Otter not to play by the river unless there is someone there to watch you!"

"But the elders are watching us," Spotted Eagle said.

"Come away from there right now. The Old Ones talk of terrible things from the forbidden Ghost Canyon. You will have nightmares if you stay and listen to them."

The other mothers quickly scolded their children and steered them away from the elders. Wander shrugged her shoulders and waved at Little Otter as her mother led her and Spotted Eagle away. Wander stayed behind with Dreaming Bear and the other elders until Meadow Lark came for her.

The creature continued to hide in the willows.

Chapter 3

The Stranger from Ghost Canyon

What is Ugly?
What is Strange?
Have we all forgotten,
Who creates and rearranges?
Only feral beauty hidden deep,
Are shown to those,
Who gratefully seek.

The next day, the creature sniffed the air, sucking in the delicious smells of food cooking. After not eating for several days, its hunger drove it out of its hiding place. It paddled to the edge of the river where it heard the people talking not too far away from their village.

"What is that strange ugly creature thing floating in the willow boat?" one of the women asked another.

"It came from Ghost Canyon by way of the river," said another. "I'd stay away. It could be dangerous, as dangerous as the canyon itself."

The creature looked like an uprooted and burnt-out tree. When it got out of its boat it shook itself like a wet dog. Hair matted and twisted into knots covered its muddy head. Its face was that of a boy child, dark and blackened with smoke, his body covered in mud and roots. He could not speak, but made wild animal sounds and bird whistles. He howled like a coyote and cocked his head to the side listening for someone to respond.

He screeched, he yelped, he croaked and barked and got everyone's attention. He sniffed at the people who quickly backed away from him. And then he poked and prodded at the children with his dirty hands. He pulled at their hair, then stuck his fingers in their mouth to see what they had been eating.

Mothers quickly gathered their children, shielding them from the creature. When they saw the strange animal-like tracks the creature made in the earth, they were frightened. Some of the people ran back to the village to get away from him. But the Old Ones…they were curious.

"He seems to know the language of the animals," Dreaming Bear explained. "He must have survived the explosion from the canyon. Let us welcome the child who has traveled far."

"We know nothing of this ugly one who comes from Ghost Canyon!" a woman shouted. "We have no use for this strange creature who cries like the ghost animals frightening our children. How do we know he is not a nightmare beast sent by the angry ghost animals to haunt our village?"

"And the set of tracks he makes are like no others, it's like he has a ghost animal who follows after him!" a man yelled out.

The boy wasn't used to the scowls and unfriendly sounds that came from some of the people. He was ready to run away when the old clay woman, Meadow Lark, approached. Wander clung tightly to her grandmother, curiously watching the boy's every move.

"Come with me, boy, and I will take you home and feed you. Maybe when we get you cleaned up…you will not look so scary to the others."

The boy followed the friendly woman and the timid little girl back to their home.

People began to whisper among themselves, "The old clay woman is good to take in the lost child Wander, but foolish to do the same for this creature of the canyon. You would think she learned her lesson when she lost her great aunt Swallow Tail to the canyon. And now this creature will be cause for more trouble. I am sure she will be sorry!"

Meadow Lark was not afraid of Ghost Canyon like the others. The closer she went up towards the canyon, the better she found the clay to be. The closer to the sacred cottonwood tree, the more magical the clay would become. And she was not afraid of the boy. His animal chatter and sounds brought back fond memories of all the animals that once were so plentiful before the explosion. She welcomed the boy and treated him as her own grandson. And so the boy made his home with Meadow Lark and Wander.

Right away the people could see he did not fit in. In the busy village the boy just got in the way. He didn't know what work was. He didn't know the first thing about how to be helpful. Instead, he ran wild like an animal tossing and chasing sticks. He splashed and played in the mud, chattering in grunts, growls, and whistles. He would have liked to play with the other children but they ran away

from him. His shrill animal cries hurt their ears
and he made scary animal faces.

"We aren't supposed to play with you," one child cried out.

"Yeah, no one wants to play with a smelly animal boy who can't talk and wallows in the mud," another said. "You can't understand us anyway. So why don't you go away and play with your animal ghost friends and leave us alone."

It was true the boy could not speak their language, but he did understand what they were saying. He drew with a willow stick in the dirt trying to show them that he did understand. He drew pictures and symbols that looked almost like an alphabet. But the children only kicked at the dirt and ran away.

The boy cried out wildly in frustrated animal sounds. Why couldn't anyone understand him?

Chapter 4

Child of Prairie Mud

What is this thing you call a dream?
Haunted Ghosts that cry?
This thing that comes to greet you
In the darkness of the night,
From high up hidden canyon walls?

Creeping, Crawling, Slivering, Stalking,
Screeching, Scrowling, Howling wildly,
Bursting, Bashing, Gnashing deep,
Into your child's most precious sleep?

What is this scary thing that has become,
Trapped deep inside the mind
Between your ears?
How is it that you have made,
These Sacred Dreams,
Your Greatest Fears?

The boy played alone. Out on the prairie he dug holes and made scary ghost-like creatures out of the mud with pointy willow sticks. The people would go out of their way so they would not trip and fall into one of the holes.

The people called him "Mud Boy, one who digs holes in the earth where scary, horrible nightmare creatures escape and creep into the night."

But the Old Ones viewed him differently.

"Mud Boy is a child of prairie mud. He hears stories from the earth he digs and shapes," Dreaming Bear said. "We believe his roots are still strongly connected to the earth like the sacred cottonwood tree. We believe he has the gift to dream. It is shameful that our own children do not even know what a dream is and have never had one. Maybe someday the Mud Boy will learn to speak our language and share his dreams with our people. Maybe he will teach our children what a dream is. Then someday they might know Animal Wisdom."

"The only thing Mud Boy can do is run around like a wild animal scaring our children away. He doesn't speak, he growls. He doesn't play like normal children do. He creeps, he crawls, he slithers and stalks like an animal beast always ready to attack." A disgruntled man cried out: "Nobody dreams anymore so why should our children know what a dream is? There is no need for them to bother."

Secretly Wander and Little Otter disagreed with the disgruntled man. They alone were curious and wanted to know more about dreams.

"I watch Mud Boy when he sleeps at night. And sometimes I think he must go to wonderful places," Wander whispered in Little Otter's ear. "I don't think he has nightmares like we do. He is always happy when he wakes up in the morning. When I have nightmares, I always wake up grumpy."

"Where do you think he goes when he dreams?" asked Little Otter.

"I'm not sure, but wherever it is…I think he must fly to get there."

"Why do you say that?"

"Because sometimes I'll be watching him sleep at night and he'll be flapping his arms like a bird. Then all of a sudden he just seems to disappear into the night. When I look outside I see some animal running away. I know it must be him because he makes those funny sounds. You know those squeals he makes, like he's calling out to someone or some animal?"

"Ooooooh," swooned Little Otter. "More than anything else I'd like to have a dream."

"So would I," Wander said, her voice trailing off. "So would I."

Their desire to know more about dreams won over fear as Wander and Little Otter watched Mud Boy. And with the two of them together, they had the courage to stay and observe the scary mud figures being made. The girls even discovered they too liked to make shapes in the mud. They hoped that by watching Mud Boy and making their own mud figures they might learn how to have a dream themselves. But as hard as they tried, they could not make mud creatures so fierce and real as Mud Boy's. There was something different about Mud Boy's creatures, something that made them almost lifelike in a beautiful, yet scary sort of way.

As each day passed there were more things that made Mud Boy so very different than the rest of the children. While the other children played and learned together, Mud Boy was off by himself seeing and listening to things that the other people could not see or hear. He tried to share with the people and show them what he knew by drawing strange symbols resembling an alphabet and pictures in the dirt. Still they did not understand. Frustrated, he began to make more and more mud creatures. The more frustrated the boy became the deeper he dug the holes and the bigger and scarier the mud creatures grew!

"Mud Boy not only speaks the language of animals, I believe he is communicating with the ghost animals up in the canyon," one man said to another. "Look at these ugly mud creatures he makes. They look like my worst nightmare. Look at the animal tracks that follow him everywhere. One of these days I believe those ghost animals are going to take their revenge out on us."

"Maybe, but maybe he might be trying to tell us something like the elders say," the other man said. "Whatever it is, it's just too mysterious for us to understand."

"I wonder who it is that Mud Boy talks to that knows his animal language," Little Otter whispered.

"Maybe it is the Dream Spirits the elders talk about," Wander replied. "I think the only way to find out is if I go and follow him while he is dreaming at night. That way I might see where he goes to. Maybe I'll see who he talks to. Maybe…I'll even have a dream!"

"Can I go with you, Wander? I want a dream too!"

Chapter 5

The Story of Swallow Tail

In the night dark and deep,
I take the land within my wings,
Wherever dreams may go,
Wherever they will take me,
I am not afraid to go.

Come to us, Early Morn,
Awake the sky with warm Red-Orange.
I have taken these fine colors for my fur.
My paws run black
Upon the smoke black ash.
My colors change with every season,
Wherever dreams may go,
Wherever they will take me,
I am not afraid to go.

"My family will be making a two-day trip with some of the others out to the forest to gather pine nuts and berries," Little Otter told Wander. "My mother says I can stay with you if I keep out of trouble. And only if Mud Boy sleeps out side away from us. Now I can go with you and get a dream too!"

The first night Meadow Lark gave each of the girls and Mud Boy a pinch of clay. "Special clay for a special occasion," she said. "This is the clay I have saved back when Swallow Tail took me with her to dig for clay. This was many years ago when I was about your age. It is the clay the Dream Spirits like the most. When you shape something from it and offer it to the Dream Spirits as a gift, they will bring you a dream."

"I will make my clay into the animal I see at night," said Wander.

"I will make my clay into a dream," said Little Otter.

The clay seemed to magically shape itself into whatever each child desired.

When Mud Boy was given his special piece of clay he ran away with it and hid himself in the willows.

The second night Meadow Lark built a small fire with the dried dung of many hoofed animals. She asked the children to bring their finished clay pieces so they could be put in the fire.

"Won't our clay pieces burn up in the fire?" asked Little Otter. The worried expression on Mud Boy's face showed he too was concerned.

"Many things do burn up in the fire but not the clay from the earth," Meadow Lark replied.

"The heat from the fire will make the clay glow like a star out in the night. When the fire has died out in the morning, your clay pieces will be hard as rock and the mud color it is now will be transformed into a rust red-orange color—you will see. This is what our people discovered from Swallow Tail and her friend."

Meadow Lark smiled and carefully placed the girls' pieces in the fire. Mud Boy did the same but would not let anyone see his piece.

The fire slowly went to work creating its glowing magic over the three clay pieces. And while the girls stayed huddled close together with Meadow Lark, Mud Boy watched wide-eyed.

"Who was Swallow Tail?" asked Little Otter.

"Swallow Tail was my great aunt. She and her best friend Wander used to play at the bottom of the canyon when they were young girls. They watched the birds take pieces of clay from the banks near the edge of the river to build their nests," Meadow Lark explained.

"I was named after Wander, her best friend, wasn't I, Grandmother?" Wander proudly said. "And Little Otter and I are best friends."

"Yeah, we are just like Swallow Tail and Wander. We make things in the magic clay for the Dream Spirits so we will have a dream," Little Otter said.

"Yes, and soon the both of you will be joining the women in making clay into pottery," Meadow Lark said.

"Grandmother, please tell us the rest of the story of Swallow Tail and the birds who made the clay nests," said Wander.

Meadow Lark continued, "The pieces of clay the birds used to make their nests clung safely high up in the canyon cliffs. And every year the birds gave birth to many hatchlings. The girls learned quickly how to find clay and make nest shapes of their own by watching the birds. As the girls grew older and became young women they began to make bigger and more beautiful shaped nests that looked more like the pots we use today. But the people thought they were foolishly wasting their time because the clay easily crumbled and could not hold water without turning into mud.

"One year, the year of the explosion, a fire broke loose over the canyon, destroying everything in its path. Most of the people and animals were able to escape but it killed many of our young animals, who could not yet run or fly away. Swallow Tail tried to save the hatchlings before the fire could get to them. Some say she fell to her death trying to climb the steep canyon wall to save them. Some say she became one with the birds and flew away with the hatchlings up into the canyon to the last sacred cottonwood tree. There were no remains of her body. Instead, left at the bottom of the high canyon cliffs were the mud-clay pots Swallow Tail and Wander had made. The fire had transformed the mud-colored pots into a rust red-orange color that had become hard as rock. It was discovered that the pots when fired became strong and sturdy vessels that could hold the river water.

"Our people believed that the hatchlings sacrificed their lives to share the secret of the fired mud-clay vessels. They were grateful and named the birds after Swallow Tail."

"What happened to her best friend, Wander?" asked Little Otter.

"Yeah, did she fly away too?" Wander added.

"Some people believe Wander lost her way up in the canyon searching for Swallow Tail. Some say the angry ghost animals kept her prisoner. No one knows for sure. Sometimes I can hear her voice calling out, 'Swallow Tail, Swallow Tail come home, Swallow Tail. Our people no longer think we are foolish. The fire has made our mud-clay pots strong and they now hold the river water. Please come home, Swallow Tail. They have even named the birds after you.'"

Mud Boy, who had been listening quietly, could not hold back his excitement. He jumped up and began flapping his arms like a bird. He swooped low and pecked at the ground with his mouth and then leaped up into the air.

"Mud Boy is the swallow bird, gathering the mud-clay and flying up into the sky, flying up to the cliffs to make his nests," Wander cheered. The girls clapped in time as Mud Boy danced around the fire imitating the swallow.

After the fire burned down a ways, the girls made their way to their mats on the floor inside the mud-clay hut and pretended to be asleep. Outside, Mud Boy watched the fire.

Shortly after Meadow Lark nodded off, Wander looked out the window. The light of the full moon shone upon the blanket of prairie stretching from one end of the horizon to the other. A looping path of water lit as bright as the moon cut gently through the land. Only the dark shadows from Ghost Canyon seem to keep the prairie and its river from falling off the edge of the earth and out into the night sky. Mud Boy, tucked safely upon his bed of earth, slept soundly unaware he was being watched.

"Little Otter, it's time, Mud Boy is making flying motions in his sleep."

Quietly, the girls tiptoed out the door. By the time they were outside, all they could see was a small dog the color of rust red-orange running and bounding away. It was running so fast and bounding so high above the prairie grass it leaped up into the air transforming itself into a bird-like creature flying away to the canyon. Without a word being said the girls went chasing after it. But soon they found themselves deep in the middle of a thicket of tall willows. The light of the moon flickered in and out of the swaying branches and leaves. The further into the thicket of willows the more lost they became.

"Why do you chase after me?" a voice suddenly came from the willows.

The girls both let out a shriek and grabbed on to one another. Cautiously they looked around to see who spoke to them but were unable to see where the voice was coming from.

"Why do you chase after me?" it asked again.

Finally after several trembling moments Wander cleared her voice to speak. "We were ch-ch-chasing after Mud Boy to see where he g-g-goes to get his dreams."

"We are looking for a dream so we might have our own story to tell," added Little Otter.

"Silly girls, you have to be asleep in order for

the Dream Spirits to bring you a dream. You can't be running around in the willows and expect to be given a dream."

"But when we are asleep the Dream Spirits only bring us nightmares."

The willows began to rustle.

"Listen to the one you call Mud Boy and some-day you will have dreams of your own."

"But we cannot understand Mud Boy's animal language. No one can understand what he is trying to say…not even Dreaming Bear."

"Listen to the one you call Mud Boy," the voice said again and faded away into the willows. "And someday there will be dreams enough for everyone."

The willows separated with a zigzag pattern, never revealing a face for the voice.

"Did you see where he went to?" Little Otter asked breathlessly.

"I couldn't see anything. I think we were talk-ing to a g-g-ghost."

"Oh no! If my mama finds out I've been talk-ing to a ghost she'll know it had to do with Mud Boy. We better get back home before Meadow Lark wakes up and finds us missing. If I get into trouble I'll never get to find a dream."

"And whatever we do, we shouldn't talk about this to anyone!"

When the girls found their way out of the willows they ran back to the village. And there near the fire slept Mud Boy as if he had never moved at all!

Chapter 6

The Hunting Trip

How can it be,
That I have gathered all,
My feral kin to this unhappy day?
For some of us were created,
To give our life away,
While other hungry mouths are fed.
But oh Great Spirit hear me now,
I have no heart,
From where I stand,
To throw away,
Those lives not meant to eat,
Nor those,
Whose first breath,
Have not yet been taken.

The next morning Wander and Little Otter almost forgot about the night before. Excitedly they collected their clay objects from the cooled fire ring. They joined Mud Boy and danced around on the prairie with their transformed clay pieces, flapping their arms, flying like the swallows.

When Little Otter's family returned from the pine nut and berry gathering they were tired. Hungry Hunter and Spotted Eagle took the baskets to the plaza while Little Otter's mother came to get her.

"Mama, come see what I made with the magic clay!" Little Otter sang out.

But before her mother could reach her, Little Otter fell into one of the holes Mud Boy had made. Tangled up in the midst of the mud creatures, Little Otter flailed about with willow sticks poking out of her like a porcupine. The fall had broken her leg.

After a couple of days Meadow Lark and Wander went to see how Little Otter was doing. But they were not welcomed. Outside the door Little Otter's mother drew a crowd of people as she began to speak in a loud voice.

"Mud Boy's creatures have attacked my child. She has a high fever and has become ill with fright and will not come out from hiding," the frantic mother cried out. "I say this boy is a danger to us all."

Then Little Otter's mother looked over at Meadow Lark and Wander with squinty eyes. "And I no longer feel that it is wise for Little Otter to have anything to do with Mud Boy or those who have anything to do with him. Since the sleepover, Little Otter has been plagued with nightmares. She talks crazy talk about some magical rust red-orange dog that has run off to Ghost Canyon. She talks about some dream she has lost!"

Wander buried her face in her grandmother's skirt unable to hide her tears. She closed her fist tightly around the rust red-orange clay piece Little Otter had made, the clay piece that dropped out of her hand when she fell into the hole.

"We never know what Mud Boy is up to," an angry woman added. "What will become of our children if he is allowed to create these mud monsters that harm our children?"

The people gathered up sticks and stones as they made their way out onto the prairie flats. They yelled and screamed and threw the objects at the ugly mud creatures until they crumbled into great big heaps of dirt.

Even the old ones agreed that Mud Boy should not be allowed to dig holes that someone could get hurt in.

"Mud Boy needs something he can do that will keep him out of trouble," Dreaming Bear said. "He has a lot of energy, if we could just think of a way to put it to good use."

Just then Hungry Hunter pushed his way through the crowd of people, and yelled out, "Since Mud Boy knows Animal Wisdom maybe we can use him. We have gathered only small amounts of pine nuts and berries, and the fish are becoming scarce in the river. Soon we will not have enough to keep us all alive. We need to find a place where we can go hunting. For many of our boys it will be their first hunt," Hungry Hunter said stretching an arm towards the older boys.

"Mud Boy is old enough to come with us. We can take him along with the other boys to the forest to hunt. He might prove himself to be useful since he knows the language of the animals. He can show us where to find them."

The people all agreed.

Mud Boy was eager to please the people. He

was happy to go with the hunters and hopefully prove his usefulness.

Several miles outside the village the men and boys traveled, following Mud Boy. Animals began to appear. As the hunting party came closer to the forest, the animals began to appear from everywhere, some the hunters had not seen for many years.

Animals came from the deepest parts of the forest to share greetings with Mud Boy. Herds of buffalo, deer, elk and moose, and flocks of duck and geese began to show. The hunters were amazed at the number of animals who showed no fear of Mud Boy. And what was even more amazing, the cougars, wolves, and other beasts of prey came up to Mud boy and he showed no fear of them.

"We shall have so much meat to bring back to the village, we will never go hungry," one boy yelled out. "We will all be heroes!"

"Not if the beasts of prey get them first. I say we shoot them all!" a hunter said and drew back his arrow.

"Get out of the way Mud Boy," he said, and carelessly they began shooting their arrows and throwing their spears at any and all of the animals in sight.

Frightened, Mud Boy and the animals all ran or flew away.

When the people lost their dreams, they forgot their pact with the animals. They forgot their Animal Wisdom. When the hunters had dreams, they were told which animal they could hunt and which ones they could not. When that animal was killed, the hunter would thank the animal for giving up its life so that his people could live another day. And they never took more than they could use.

Eagerly the hunting party set up camp, not once thinking about where Mud Boy may have run off. They were in such a hurry to get their bows and arrows and spears ready for the next day to hunt that they didn't bother with the animals they had already brought down.

The next day came and went. It wasn't long before all of the hunters knew something was terribly wrong.

"I don't like what is going on here," said one hunter. "Today not one of us has brought down a single deer. Not even our best archer has come close to his target!"

"And where are all the animals we brought down the day before? said another. "We have searched everywhere for them and cannot find them. They have all vanished!"

A group of boys whispered among themselves, pointing in the direction Mud Boy had run.

"It is Mud Boy, who is making the animals disappear!" Spotted Eagle cried out. "With the power of his animal language he is able to warn them to run or fly away from us."

The men began to grumble. "The boy is some kind of a mud witch with all of his strange powers."

Another frightened hunter yelled out, "For all we know he could be communicating with the cougar, the wolf or bear, all the flesh-eating animals of the forest! They could be joining with him and the ghost animals of the canyon and planning an attack on our men and boys. I say we leave before he causes some serious trouble!"

The men and boys quickly packed up and left the forest. Mud Boy followed the hunting party back to the village, all the while trying to stay out of their sight.

When the hunters returned to the village the people ran to greet them. But they knew something was wrong.

"Mud Boy has used his power of animal language against us. He has made the animals disappear," one boy said. "We have no meat for our people because of him."

Seeing the hunters empty handed, the hungry

village people became angry. Mud Boy shook with fear as he was grabbed from out of the willows where he had been hiding. The people crowded around him wanting an explanation.

He desperately tried to show the people with pictures he drew in the dirt. He tried to show the angry people the reason for doing what he did. But how could he draw a picture of the pact between the people and animals, the pact that the people were now dishonoring? How could he make them understand the dreams of Animal Wisdom, the dreams that had been taken away from them?

The people shouted and yelled at Mud Boy, calling him a mud witch. They kicked the dirt at him and made ugly faces.

From then on, if anything went wrong, it would be the Mud Witch Boy they would blame.

Chapter 7

The Path of Mud-Clay

This is mud-clay
Where dreams can take shape,
In my hands I create.

Give life to this creation Oh Great Spirit,
Connect me to all things in beauty,
From sweet Mother Earth.

To keep order and peace in the village the Old Ones called for a meeting.

"I say we tie the mud witch to a boulder and go back into the forest to hunt. That way he won't be able to follow us and make the animals disappear," one of the young hunters said.

"Better yet, banish him from our village!"

"No, no that won't work. A mud witch with powers like his could be twice as bad if he joins with the ghost animals up in the canyon to haunt us in the night."

People were talking all at once until no one in particular could be heard. The Old Ones tried to get the crowd's attention so that the old clay woman Meadow Lark could speak.

"RRRRRRRAAAAAAaaaarrrrrrr !" Mud Boy shrieked. His loud blood-curdling mountain-lion roar quickly silenced the crowd. The people cowered and hung on to one another. They began to pay attention.

In a gentle but firm voice, the old clay woman Meadow Lark began to speak, "I say we give Mud Boy another chance to prove himself."

"Foolish old woman, why should he be given another chance?" an angry woman yelled out. "No one can trust the Mud Witch Boy."

Mud Boy let out a warning: "Grrrrrr."

The angry woman backed away into the crowd and did not say another word.

"Let him go with me so I may show him where to dig for clay," Meadow Lark began again. "When Swallow Tail went up towards the canyon she always brought back the best clay. Since the explosion, no one will go near the canyon. But Mud Boy is not afraid.

"Let Mud Boy help me carry the clay back and prepare it for the other women and young girls to shape their pottery. My hands are getting too old and tired to be digging in the earth and my back too weak to carry the load. The steep path of mud-clay is becoming difficult for me to walk. One day I will not be able to carry on this task and we will need someone to take my place. I will teach Mud Boy the path of mud-clay and show him how to shape it into something useful. And I will make sure he covers his holes so no one will fall in again."

"I agree with Meadow Lark," one of the pottery-making woman said. "We need some good clay to teach our young girls the art of making pottery vessels."

"Yeah, and this should keep the mud witch out of trouble," another said. "I can't imagine he could cause any more problems than he has already. Besides, no one else will go near the dreaded canyon. And if anything bad should happen it should happen to the mud witch since he caused the trouble."

"Let him dig for clay and prepare it for the women to make their pottery," the people cheered.

"After all, he digs holes in the earth to make his nightmare monsters. Why not make his digging useful?"

The village people laughed and finally agreed.

And once again Mud Boy was eager to please the people. He followed the old clay woman Meadow Lark up the mud-clay path towards Ghost Canyon.

Traveling to the edges of the river and arroyos below the canyon, Mud Boy quickly learned which parts of the earth could be used for clay. Steadily, day after day he dug and gathered the clay. For the first time the village people were pleased with him. The old clay woman Meadow Lark was proud of Mud Boy and sang the Path of Mud-Clay song just for him.

This is the path of mud-clay upon which I walk,
And from the souls of my feet,
I can hear the earth sing her stories to me.
With river rush cattail, water and sand,
I mix into clay.
Kneading over and over,
Till all things are connected,
Till all things are one.

This is mud-clay,
Where dreams can take shape,
In my hands I create.

Give life to this creation Oh Great Spirit,
Connect me to all things in beauty,
From sweet Mother Earth.

After the clay had been dug and hauled back to the village, it was laid out to dry in the sun. Afterward, it was pounded into a fine powder. To the powdered clay just the right amount of river water was added and mixed. Then sand was added to give it strength and cattail fiber added to hold it together. After the clay was kneaded into rounded balls, it was covered with wet rags. The clay was set aside until the women would shape it into pottery.

On the plaza near the large stumps of dead cottonwood trees the young girls learned to coil ropes of clay. Pinching and shaping, they formed small cups and bowls. And for the first time in several weeks Little Otter finally limped out of her home to join the others. Her mother kept close watch over her and kept her far away from Mud Boy.

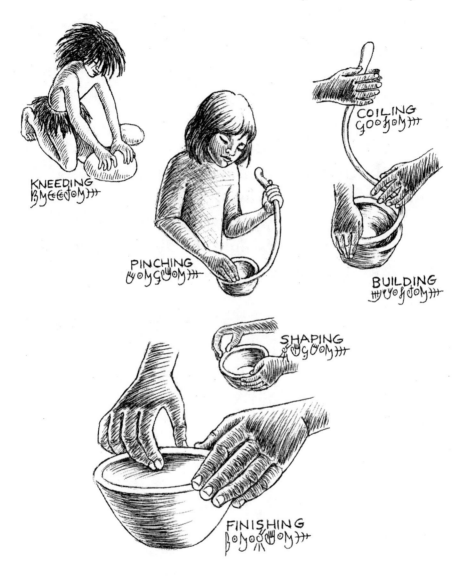

KNEEDING

PINCHING

COILING

BUILDING

SHAPING

FINISHING

"Little Otter," Wander cried out, trying to get her friend's attention. But Little Otter would not look up. She kept her eyes down listening and watching only her mother.

Mud Boy barked and howled and hummed the song he learned from the old clay woman. And although his hands were strong for digging and he could make ugly mud monsters, he had difficulty with the task of making the shape of a bowl. He couldn't keep the walls of the clay centered and even. Everything he made was crooked and lop-sided and toppled all over.

When the young girls saw all of his mistakes and the clay all over himself, his face, and in his hair, they laughed and made fun of him.

"Mud Witch, Mud Witch, Mud Witch Boy,
Will never grow up.
Dirty, stinky, noisy, crude,
Clumsy, dumbsy,
Mud Witch Boy,

He walks, he talks,
He plays with ghosts,
Wallowing in mud from head to toe,
Mud Witch, Mud Witch,
Mud Witch Boy!"

The boys in the village gathered to watch Mud Boy. They joined with the girls in their teasing and added their own words.

"Mud Witch, Mud Witch, Mud Witch Boy,
Can't prove himself brave,
He runs from danger,
Into trouble,
Mud Witch, Mud Witch,
Mud Witch Boy.

Up in the canyon,
One day he'll get lost.
Stuck in the mud,
Or eaten alive.
Mud Witch, Mud Witch, Mud Witch Boy!"

Mud Boy didn't let the teasing stop him. Long after the people went home he stayed behind well into the night struggling to make a simple bowl. And all the while, he hummed and growled and hummed and yelped. He hummed and yodeled and howled up to the moon. He howled and hummed to the tune of the old clay woman Meadow Lark's song.

Chapter 8

Broken Shards and Animal Tracks

Broken shards and animal tracks,
I have no other way,
But scratching lines and scratching signs,
These are my messages
In clay.
Can you hear me,
Through my words?
Can't you see,
My need to say?

The next morning the village people woke up early to the sounds of many animal sounds. Dreaming Bear looked out side his door and spoke to the old clay woman Meadow Lark and Wander as they walked by.

"Did you hear all the sounds of the animals last night? It was like the time when we used to dream," he said.

"Oh yes, but I think that it was just Mud Boy. He stayed up humming and howling after everyone had left way into the night, trying to shape a bowl," the woman replied.

"There were too many sounds for one child to make," Dreaming Bear said. "Look there on the ground! There are tracks of many animals."

The people followed the tracks to the plaza.

"It looks as though a large herd of animals has come right through the middle of the village," a terrified woman cried out.

The people gasped in disbelief. Everywhere, clay bowls and cups were broken and scattered. Lumps of prepared clay had been trampled and splattered all about. Walls near the plaza were broken down into crumbling ruins. The young girls who had just made their first cups and bowls the day before found only heaps of broken shards.

"These are not the tracks of animals. These are the tracks of the mud monsters created by the Mud Witch. I believe he was in charge of this whole outrage," Hungry Hunter yelled out. "There he is sleeping right in the middle of this horrible mess."

The people began shouting and shaking their fists. Mud Boy woke up in a terrible fright.

"The Mud Witch Boy's monsters have come to destroy all of us and our village too! They have all been unleashed and have come to get their revenge on our people."

Dreaming Bear frowned as he bent over the broken pottery. He traced his fingers over the small pictures and symbols that were scratched onto the clay shards. He tried to understand the message Mud Boy made in the shards. He tried to remember symbols and pictures from his long-ago dreams. He tried to study every little detail, in order to figure out why Mud Boy would take part in destroying the pottery and plaza walls.

After going through the rubble, Dreaming Bear carefully picked up two pieces of curiously shaped clay. The clay was the color of rust red-orange. When he put the pieces together they made the shape of a child riding a red fox. He hushed the noisy girls and angry crowd.

"Who has made this fine looking mud-clay figure?" he asked.

There was complete silence. Mud Boy shyly sat up on his haunches and tapped his fist against his chest.

The old clay woman Meadow Lark and several others came to look at the clay figure of the child riding a red fox. They agreed that the boy had a special gift that they had never seen before.

"Child of prairie mud," Dreaming Bear called out. "The one who hears stories in the earth he shapes has foretold of the dreams to come. Last night for the first time in many years, I was visited by the child who rides the red fox."

"Foolish old man, you know that no one has dreams any more," another man said. "This is just another attack on our village by the Mud Witch. The only things he can make are these ugly nightmare mud monsters that have taken on a life of their own. They now have come to take their revenge and destroy our village."

"No, noooo! Please listen to me. What Dreaming Bear says is true," Little Otter cried out. She looked to Wander and Meadow Lark for reassurance and then spoke directly to the crowd. "I saw a boy jump upon the back of the red fox and chase my nightmares away. They were huge, horrible, nightmares that would not let me go. But the boy and the red fox chased them all around the village. It was the angry nightmares who came crashing through the walls destroying all the pottery…not Mud Boy. The boy and red fox chased the nightmares away from the village and out towards the canyon. When they saw the nightmares were gone they sang to the moon. I know that it is true because I saw them."

The village people crowded around to see the rust red-orange clay figure. Some of the people wanted to believe that Mud Boy made it. But most of the people could not.

"If you made the boy riding a red fox, surely you can make another one just like it," a woman said and handed Mud Boy a piece of clay.

In front of all the people Mud Boy tried to shape another figure. His hands trembled as he shaped the clay. The more the people stared at him and grumbled, the more his hands would tremble. The more the people failed to believe in his ability, the more he failed at making the boy riding the red fox.

"Mud Boy is not the one who has made the clay figure!" the woman shouted. "He is a mud witch and troublemaker. He is not one of us. We don't need any more trouble and we don't need any dreams. Dreams are only for those foolish enough to have them."

"I say the Mud Witch Boy should be sent away and never allowed to return unless he can prove himself by going up into Ghost Canyon and destroying all of our nightmares. If he can do this and come back alive then he must go and bring back all of the animals from the forest so that we may hunt again," Hungry Hunter announced.

Many of the people yelled and chased Mud Boy up towards the canyon. They chased him as far as they were brave enough to go.

Distressed, Mud Boy ran away. Wander and Little Otter wondered if he would ever try to return to the village after the way the people treated him.

Chapter 9

A Voice in the Wilderness

My feral voice you hear,
In grunts, growls, and whistles,
But only animals can understand.

Please, Great Spirit, give me voice,
The whole Universe can Understand.
A simple song to travel far,
Throughout the prairie land.

Mud Boy walked along the river. Many stories came to him as he walked barefooted upon the cool wet earth. The stories came to him from the dreams he remembered. And now he hummed the song the old clay woman Meadow Lark had taught him. He hummed with a mournful howl.

He made mud-clay animals, silently saying a prayer for each animal's wisdom to return to the people. He made every animal he had ever seen then set them alongside the path of the river. If only there was a way he could share his dreams of Animal Wisdom. If only there was a way he could bring back the animals so his people would not go hungry.

The voices that no one else could hear began to remind him, "Mud Boy, it is time for you to become what you were always meant to be. Take now your boat made of willow and follow the river up into Ghost Canyon. Going against the current of the mighty river will be the most difficult task you will do. But this is what must be done to fight off the nightmares of all of the village people. This is what you must do to find the mud-clay that sparkles with the light of star shine. This is the clay that if your shape is true, will bring back the dreams to all the village people."

Just before he came to the canyon he began to hear horrible monster sounds and screams from the animal ghosts. They growled and howled and screeched and moaned. They surrounded him with a heavy mist of dark and gloom. Mud Boy covered his ears but the horrible noise would not go away. Bravely as he could he let out a growl. When that didn't work he let out his biggest, fiercest and loudest "GR-R-R-R-R-R-R-R-R-O-O-O-O-O-W-L!" But that made the horrible monsters and ghost animals angry. Their eyes bulged in all directions looking for the sound that came from the boy in his boat.

"Who do you think you are waking us up and disturbing our sleep?"

"Don't you know who you are dealing with? We are the nightmares of the village people. Not just one, not just two—we are the nightmares of all the village people. And there are many!"

As they spoke their toxic breath spewed forth a violent windstorm. The storm gathered up the mud and debris along the riverbank and began hurling itself around, pummeling everything in its path. The willows became lashing whips striking out and entangling Mud Boy. Mud Boy fought as best he could. He dodged the mud and debris. He used his paddle to defend himself against the willows that whipped at his flesh. But he was no match for the angry monsters and ghost animals.

"You are foolish to try to fight us. Why, you are nothing but a boy." They screamed and yelled.

Boulders rolled heavily in the water, colliding with one another and stirring up the river into raging waves nearly swallowing Mud Boy. Yet as tired as he was he managed to ride out the angry nightmare storm. He couldn't let them see that his weak and tired body could not take it anymore.

When the nightmares saw that despite their best efforts the boy was still afloat in his willow boat, they began to bargain with him.

"Why don't you join us, boy, instead of trying to fight us off? You know we will never let you get out of the canyon alive. Come with us and take your revenge out upon the people who have turned you away from their village."

Mud Boy shook his head wearily from side to side.

"Come with us and join our nightly haunts. And if you do…we will make you strong and powerful just like us."

When Mud Boy thought he had no other choice he saw a tiny sliver of light on the edge of the riverbank. In the light a red fox sat yipping in a small sad voice. When Mud Boy reached out for the fox in the light he was quickly sucked up into the darkness of the nightmares. As he spun around, almost out of control, he heard a child's voice begin to sing.

He looked all around to see where it was coming from. But all he could see was fire and blackness beyond. All of the village people's most horrible and terrible nightmares were staring and glaring down at him. He searched for the child's singing voice until he could search no more.

Suddenly from the river he could hear the voice again, this time a soft rumbling in his ears and in his throat. When he looked down, deep into the river he found his own reflection. The singing voice belonged to him. He sang the song the old clay woman Meadow Lark had sung just for him. He sang in the language of the village people. He sang with a voice loud and clear.

His singing silenced the horrible sounds of the monsters and screaming ghosts. Into the fire and blackness they all quickly disappeared. And instead of nightmares, animals began to appear. The very animals he had shaped in clay.

By nightfall every animal he had ever known and shaped in clay began to follow him alongside the river. Their paws and hooves moved swiftly and silently, hardly touching the surface of the ground. The animals were enchanted by Mud Boy's singing voice. Eagerly they followed him all the way up into the canyon.

High above them as far as they could see was the last standing sacred cottonwood tree. The topmost branches disappeared into the sky. Its roots held deeply into the earth around the hollow of a cave. Stardust lit up the path and showed him the way.

When Mud Boy came to the tree he jumped out of the willow boat and greeted the majestic tree with his song. Underneath the trunk of the tree a light revealed the opening of the cave. Silvery stardust glittered from within a small pond. Mud Boy's voice echoed inside the hollow. As he sang he scooped up clay from the edges of the water, adding stardust. He kneaded it into the clay until all of the stories from the earth and all the dreams from the heaven were connected, till all things were one. With the handful of clay he began to shape the last creature: The Dream Spirit.

The animals gathered together at the entrance of the cave to watch the mud-clay creature taking shape. When the clay figure was finished and dried, Mud Boy built a small fire from the fallen cottonwood branches and the dung from the hoofed animals. The fire cast a warm glow throughout the hollow of the cave within the giant sacred cottonwood tree. And from every tip of every branch new leaves started to grow, shimmering and reflecting like stars out in the night. Mud Boy carefully put the stardust mud-clay creature into the fire—the fire that would magically transform the mud-clay into a rust-red orange color and make it hard as a rock.

While the creature was being fired, every tree dweller, burrower, land rover, and cave dweller, every winged flier of the sky, every mountain climber and river swimmer, every animal from the highest mountain to every animal from the ocean's deep, came to give a part of themselves to the creature made of stardust and prairie mud-clay.

"I will share my coat of changing colors to keep with the four seasons," yipped Red Fox.

"I will share the secrets of the forest," Bobcat revealed.

Deer came and shed his antlers so the creature might have a pair of his own.

"I will share my strength of digging claws to dig deep burrows," Badger gruffed.

"I will give the gift of transformation from one form into another," Butterfly announced.

Prairie Dog barked out loud and clear with all of his many family members, "We will give the gift of teamwork so you will have the wisdom and strength in numbers."

Eagle swooped on feathered wings and touched the eyes of the small mud-clay creature, "I shall share with you my gift of sight so you may see far away, the Wisdom Sight beyond the earth's horizon."

Antelope shared his running speed. Beaver shared his knowledge of building dens and dams with willows and branches. Otter shared her joy of playfulness in water and on land.

Meadow Lark and other birds of color gave the gift of song.

Elk and other land rovers gave the gift of direction, Geese and Duck in formation, Whale and

Dolphin their aquatic songs deep within the water. All the animals of migration shared their journey on land, air, and sea.

Mountain Lion growled, "I will share my speed and strength."

Bat squealed out, "I have echolocation to find my food in the darkest night. And to the mud-clay creature I share this trait."

Javelina shared her bristle coat and nose for rooting in the earth for food.

Animals with flukes, fins, and flippers, all the animals with tails, rudders, hooves and paws and claws, every beaked and sharp-toothed animal came willingly to share with the small mud-clay creature until it had the strengths of the entire animal kingdom.

They shared their wisdom and instincts; they shared all the mysteries of the earth.

Chapter 10

Child of Stardust and Prairie Mud

Child of Stardust and Prairie Mud,
One who hears stories,
From the earth he digs and shapes,
Has been given the gift to create.
The gift of Song,
The gift to Dream.

By the time all of the animals had come to offer their gifts, the fire had slowly died down. In the early morning while the embers were still barely warm, Mud Boy picked up the clay creature and cradled him in his arms. The once mud-colored creature had turned to the color of rust-red orange, the color of fired earth, with sprinkles of starlight. Small black smoke rings made a mask around his eyes and soft gray marks tattooed him like a young spotted bobcat. The creature became flesh and bones and fur.

Slowly Mud Boy took the creature by the nape of his neck like a mountain lion would her cub, and made his way up into the sacred cottonwood tree. Steadily and carefully he climbed from branch to branch. Way up into the tree he went where the branches disappeared into the sky. And there in the crook of a limb near the top he gently placed the creature upon the abandoned nest.

Mud Boy closed his eyes and whispered, "This is the mud-clay that shines like a star, where dreams can take shape in my hands I create. Give life to this creation, oh Great Spirit. Connect me to all things in beauty, from sweet Mother Earth, and Father Sky up above."

Mud Boy breathed life into the nostrils of the clay creature and became one with him. This is how Mud Boy transformed into the Dream Spirit.

With all of the wisdom and strength of the entire animal kingdom he climbed back down the sacred cottonwood tree. Then upon the back of Red Fox, they rode out into the night. With heads held high they howled and sang,

"We bring the dreams of Animal Wisdom,
We bring the dreams to all who believe.

Come out from your hiding place little Dream Spirits.

No need to be afraid anymore.
We will protect you.
We are your family, believe in yourself."

And then it was the Dream Spirits who began to come out from everywhere. Out from underneath rocks, out of the rivers, out from every crack in the earth, from the bushes and the deepest valleys, and down from the sky they came. Swiftly hundreds of them climbed up into the last sacred cottonwood tree. They stood proudly upon the branches and sang in harmony with every living creature out over the prairie land.

"We are Dream Spirits, from Earth and from Sky.
You will not always see us,

But if you listen with your heart,
You will always hear.

We bring the dreams of Animal Wisdom.
We bring the dreams to all who believe.
Let us never forget every creature created,
We all have a Dream Story to tell."

The tiny creatures threw out cottonwood seeds from the tree. In a fluff of cotton the seeds drifted through the air along the river. Cottonwood saplings began to grow everywhere the wind blew the seeds. Hundreds of cottonwood trees grew from the earth in the canyon, and all alongside the river as far as one could see. Once again, stars began to collect up in the branches of all the sacred cottonwood trees.

When the animals began to return to the village, the people knew Mud Boy had succeeded. And once again the Dream Spirits brought dreams to the animals and people.

The child they once called Mud Witch Boy is a legend and hero and is now called "Child of Star Dust and Prairie Mud, one who sings stories from the earth he shapes."

Epilogue

Little Otter and Wander have taken the place of Meadow Lark, the old clay woman. They dig for the clay around the canyon. And on special occasions they take some from the clay cave hidden deep in the roots of the sacred cottonwood tree. They sing the Path of Mud-Clay in honor of Mud Boy. Their pottery and sculptures are inspired by their dreams and the nature and animals that surround them. Dreaming Bear, Meadow Lark, and some of the elders now take their place among the stars where spirits sometime wander.

Hungry Hunter hunts only for what his people need. Through his dreams he knows which animal can be taken. For those animals that have given their life, he always gives a blessing.

Spotted Eagle didn't follow in the footsteps of his father. Still, Hungry Hunter is proud of his son. Spotted Eagle took after Dreaming Bear, and became one of the greatest storytellers ever. His epic dreams always give the children of the village stories of the earth and Animal Wisdom. Yet his most favorite story of all is about the boy who came to their village and could only speak in grunts, growls, and whistles.

Once a year when the stars are shining at their brightest, the people are visited by the boy riding the red fox. When they hear a child's voice singing from the canyon, they are reminded of the boy who courageously fought off their nightmares and bravely brought back their dreams. In this way, the people made peace with all the creatures of the canyon and no longer lived in fear.

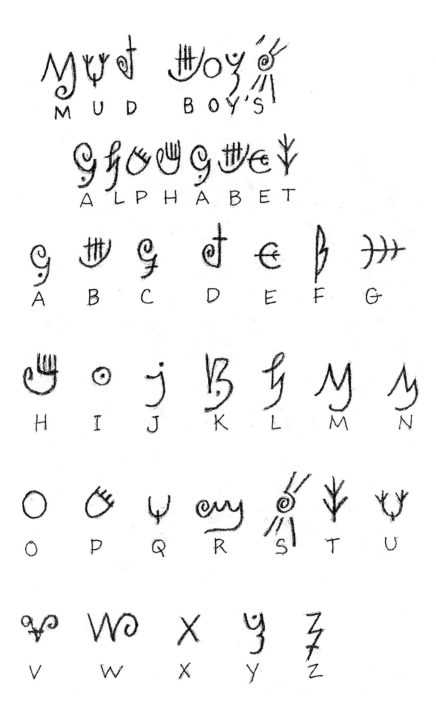

MUD BOY'S
ALPHABET

A B C D E F G

H I J K L M N

O P Q R S T U

V W X Y Z

Job 12: 7-13

But ask now the beasts, and they shall teach thee;
  and the fowls of the air, and they shall tell thee:
Or speak to the earth, and it shall teach thee: and
  the fishes of the sea shall declare unto thee.
Who knoweth not in all these that the hand of the
  Lord hath wrought this?
In whose hand is the soul of every living thing,
  and the breath of all mankind.
Doth not the ear try words? and the mouth taste
  his meat?
With the ancient is wisdom; and in length of days
  understanding.
With him is wisdom and strength, he hath counsel
  and understanding.

Valerie Temple

The events, characters, places and circumstances in the story *Mud Witch Boy of Ghost Canyon* are fictional. Any similarities to a place or any person living or dead are purely coincidental.

Similar circumstances of other peoples or places, I believe, have come from what Carl Jung calls "the collective unconscious." There are important dream symbols and persons, places, and events which, even though they may be ancient, have found a way to surface again in another form.

As I interpret them, Joseph Campbell's ideas of the importance of past, the origins of all existences being reflected in myths, and world religions being similar in mythology and originating as a dream reflect in my thinking. *Mud Witch Boy of Ghost Canyon* is a collection of my own dream fragments connected with a little imagination.

Since my concerns for the environment leave a significant impression on my psyche, many of my dreams are direct results of these concerns. Dreams are a form of language that is not always fully understood yet cannot be ignored. Dreams are journeys we take to make connection with our subconscious and to realities other than our own.

About the Author

Valerie Temple was born in Colorado and began drawing pictures and sculpting in mud-clay at an early age. Like the Mud Witch Boy she enjoys telling stories from the earth she digs and shapes. Temple has done special studies in clay building at the University of California at Santa Barbara and Ventura College and employs native firing techniques in her work. She lives in Ventura, California.

Photograph by Chuck Temple